DUDLEY SCHOOLS LIBRARY AND INFORMATION SERVICE

KU-719-791

Schools Library and Information Services

S00000684345

684345   SCH
JY FUN

First published in Germany by Verlag Friedrich Oetinger, Hamburg © 2004

This edition first published in the United Kingdom in 2006 by
The Chicken House, 2 Palmer Street, Frome, Somerset, BA11 1DS
www.doublecluck.com

Text © 2004 Cornelia Funke
Illustrations © 2004 Kerstin Meyer
Translation © 2006 Oliver Latsch

All rights reserved
No part of this publication may be reproduced or transmitted or utilized in any form or by any means,
electronic, mechanical, photocopying or otherwise, without the prior permission of the publisher

The moral rights of the author and illustrator have been asserted

Printed and bound in China by Imago

British Library Cataloguing in Publication Data available
Library of Congress Cataloguing in Publication data available

Hardback ISBN: 1 905294 03 4

THE WILDEST BROTHER

Cornelia Funke

Illustrated by Kerstin Meyer

Translated by Oliver Latsch

Chicken House

2 Palmer Street, Frome, Somerset BA11 1DS

Some mornings when Ben
wakes up he is a **wild wolf**.

Or a knight.

O̶r a **monster** covered in scars.
He paints them on his face with Anna's make-up.
He always creeps very quietly into her room.
But sometimes Anna catches him.

Then she gives him a good tickling.
Anna is Ben's big sister.

Unfortunately,
big sisters know
exactly where little
brothers are ticklish.

Sometimes Ben paints red spots on to Anna's desk with her make-up. And he tells her they are blood drops from a man-eating **monster.**

And that he'll protect her.
After all, he's lionhearted and elephant-strong.

Then Anna has to hide in the wardrobe.
Without giggling.
Because giggling makes monster-hunters terribly angry.
Anna is only allowed to make monster noises.
She's really good at it.
She grunts and snorts and growls.

And Ben, lionhearted
and elephant-strong,

fetches his three plastic
swords, pumpkin-sized
water pistol and
rubber knife,

and fights until his
face turns bright red

and the man-eating monster
is as quiet as a mouse.
Then Anna can come out
of the wardrobe again.

But Ben can't wipe the red spots off Anna's desk.

Because there are still three mouldy **green ghosts** howling in the bathroom.

And Ben has to tear them to shreds and flush them down the toilet – right now.

There's also the
slime-burping monster
who loves to lick out
the pots in the kitchen.

Fearlessly Ben throws him off the balcony.

Then, using a skipping rope, Ben ties up the burglar who creeps into the house once a week.

All this fighting is exhausting! So exhausting that once Ben even knocked one of Anna's horse posters off the wall.

But Ben does protect Anna from all the foxes and wolves in the garden so Anna can pick dandelion leaves in peace for the guinea pigs.

Ben can't help Anna pick the leaves though. He has to keep an eye on the bears lurking behind the bushes. They are just waiting for the chance to gobble up such a tasty big sister.

Yes, Ben really has to fight quite a lot.
All day long in fact.
His muscles have already
grown big from it all.

But in the evening,
when Night presses
her soot black face
against the window
and the heating creaks
like the sound of a thousand
biting beetles, Ben crawls
into Anna's bed.
Then she protects him –
from Night's soot black face
and the biting beetles.

And it is sooo wonderful
to have a big strong sister.

More Picture Books by Cornelia Funke and Kerstin Meyer

A fairy tale for tomboys!

This is a satisfying variation on the usual fairy tale in which knights compete for the hand of a princess.

Nicolette Jones, SUNDAY TIMES

. . . this jolly story, illustrated cartoon style throughout with never a dull moment.

Nicholas Tucker, CAROUSEL

£5.99
1 904442 14 5

Brings out the fighting spirit in the smallest of pirates!

Feisty girls are commonplace in picture books but Pirate Girl Molly is a particularly attractive example. . . . Funke makes her feminist points with telling delicacy.

Julia Eccleshare, GUARDIAN

Chantal Wright's vigorous translation from the German reads seamlessly and does credit to Funke's amusing text with its surprise denouement.

BOOKS FOR KEEPS - Editor's choice

£5.99
1 904442 93 5

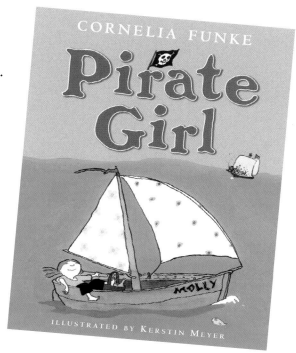

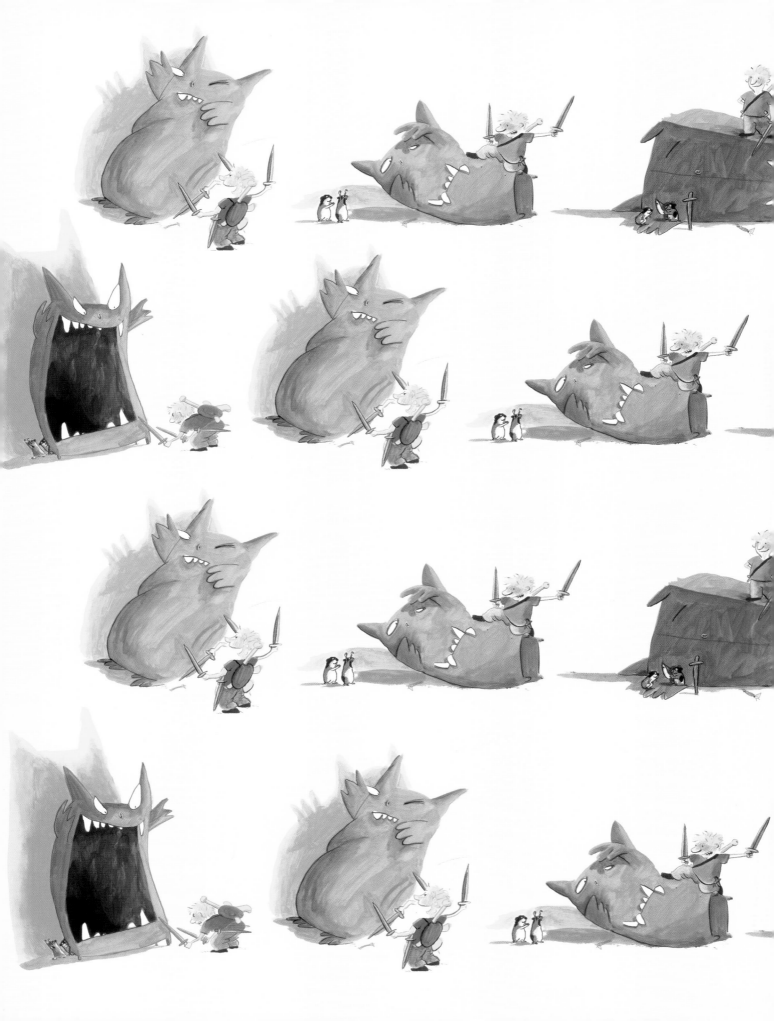